A Child's
EASTER

ISBN 0-8249-4197-7
CandyCane Press, an imprint of Ideals Publications, A Division of Guideposts
535 Metroplex Drive, Suite 250
Nashville, TN 37211
www.idealspublications.com

Printed and bound in Mexico by RR Donnelley & Sons.

Art Director, Eve DeGrie
Editorial Consultant, Karen Couch

Color separations by Precision Color Graphics, Franklin, Wisconsin

Library of Congress Cataloging-in-Publication-Data
Pingry, Patricia.
    A child's Easter / written by Patricia A. Pingry; illustrated by Stephanie McFetridge Britt.
    p. cm.
    Summary: A young boy meets Jesus at the beginning of his ministry and then witnesses the events from Jesus' triumphant entry into Jerusalem through his arrest, trial and crucifixion to his Resurrection.
    ISBN 0-8249-4197-7 (alk. paper)
    1. Jesus Christ—Passion—Juvenile fiction. 2. Jesus Christ—Resurrection—Juvenile fiction. [1. Jesus Christ—Passion—Fiction. 2. Jesus Christ—Resurrection—Fiction. 3. Easter—Fiction.] I. Britt Stephanie McFetridge, ill. II. Title.
    PZ7 .P6325 Ch 2000
    [E]—dc21   00-058638

For children everywhere, but especially for
Abigail, Benjamin, Nicholas, and Brandon Pingry;
Sarah Britt, Hannah DeGrie, and Jessica Cordona.

A Child's EASTER

By Patricia A. Pingry

Illustrated by Stephanie McFetridge Britt

AN IMPRINT OF IDEALS PUBLICATIONS, A DIVISION OF GUIDEPOSTS
NASHVILLE, TENNESSEE

I was late and running for home. Mama would be worried. When I turned the corner, I saw a man sitting beside our road. I had heard of him. He made sick children well.

Children pushed and reached out to touch him. But his friends shooed them away.

"Go home," they said. "Jesus is tired. Don't bother him."

But Jesus said, "Let the children come. Only those who believe as these children will enter heaven."

Jesus was kind. His words were gentle.

I was only four years old, but I knew that Jesus was my friend.

On my seventh birthday, we moved to Jerusalem. One spring day, I was in the marketplace when a crowd gathered.

"A parade!" I shouted and elbowed my way through the people. I looked up the road and saw a man perched on a little donkey riding down the street.

All around me, people were breaking branches off the palm trees. They waved them in the air. They fanned them toward the sky. They threw them down before the donkey. Throwing palm branches shows respect for a king.

What king rides a donkey?

Then the donkey passed right in front of me, and the man turned and smiled at me.

"Who is that man on the donkey?" asked a woman standing next to me.

"That is Jesus who heals the sick and loves little children. I met him once," I told her proudly.

Then I shouted with the crowd, "Hosanna! Hosanna to the king!"

Jesus is my king.

Four days later, Papa called me to come to him.

"Benjamin," said Papa, "I want to tell you about your friend Jesus. He and his disciples met for the Passover supper. Before they ate, Jesus washed the feet of each disciple and . . ."

"But Papa," I interrupted, "why would Jesus wash his friends' dirty feet?"

"Jesus loved his friends so much," said Papa, "that he would even stoop down and wash their feet to make them clean."

I would let Jesus make me clean.

"Before they ate," Papa continued, "Jesus broke the bread and gave them each a piece. He said to them, 'This is my body which I will give for you. Remember me.'

"Then Jesus passed around a cup and said, 'This is my blood which is shed for many.'

"Benjamin," said Papa, "we must always remember what Jesus said and did."

I'll always remember Jesus.

But Papa had more news. "Son," he said quietly, "your friend Jesus has been arrested."

"Why?" I shouted, jumping out of Papa's lap. "I saw Jesus ride into Jerusalem like a king. I threw palm branches before his donkey."

"After the Passover supper," Papa went on, "Jesus and his friends went to a garden. His friends fell asleep; but an angel was with Jesus while he prayed."

I would stay awake for Jesus.

"Soldiers came into the garden and arrested Jesus."

"Where were his friends then?" I asked. "Were they still asleep?"

"No, his friends were ready to fight," continued Papa, "but Jesus told them to stay calm. He told them that he must suffer and die to save us from our sins."

I was afraid for Jesus.

I am only seven, but I would fight for Jesus.

The next morning, Papa and I went into the city. The merchants were all whispering about Jesus.

"Jesus was questioned by the high priest," whispered a tall merchant.

"He asked Jesus, 'Are you the Christ, the Son of God?' " a fat merchant whispered.

I interrupted too loudly, "What did Jesus say?"

"He answered," whispered the fat merchant, '*I am.*' "

"I wonder what they will do to Jesus," whispered Papa.

"He is held at the governor's palace," whispered the tall merchant.

Papa and I hurried off to the palace.

I believe that Jesus is the Son of God.

Pilate, the governor, stood on the porch of the palace.

Pilate shouted, "I will release one prisoner. Do you want Jesus or Barabbas free?"

The crowd shouted, "Barabbas!"

Suddenly I was very frightened.

"Jesus!" I cried as loudly as I could. "Jesus!"

"Jesus!" called Papa. "Jesus!"

"Barabbas," chanted the crowd. "Release Ba-rab-bas. Crucify Jesus."

"Crucify him," Pilate said, and he turned and went inside.

Jesus! I will shout the name of Jesus.

I was so scared that I started to cry. Papa put his arm around my shoulders and pulled me close to him. We started walking home under the hot sun.

Suddenly the sun vanished. It was noon but as dark as midnight.

"Papa," I called. "What happened? Where is the sun?"

"Stay close to me," Papa said, taking my arm.

We started to run. I think the whole city was running.

I wonder if Jesus were scared too.

We ran into the house. Mama was huddled in a corner.

"What is happening?" she screamed. "God help us!"

Lightning lit up the sky. The earth trembled. The house began to shake.

"An earthquake!" Papa shouted. He went to the window to look outside.

"Look, Benjamin," he cried. "Three crosses stand on the hill called Golgotha. On one hangs Jesus, the Son of God, crucified for our sins. All nature cries out in sorrow."

When the earth stopped shaking, I went to bed.

I too cried for Jesus.

The next day was sunny and warm. The fat merchant came to our house with news.

"Jesus' friends took Jesus from the cross to a tomb," he said. "And a huge rock was rolled in front of the opening. A soldier is on guard to keep everybody out. No one can roll away that stone!"

We were very sad.

I missed my friend Jesus.

On Sunday morning, just as the sun was coming up, I awoke to another earthquake. By noon, the tall merchant pounded on our door.

"I have news!" he shouted. "Women went to Jesus' tomb this morning, and the guard is gone!"

The tall merchant waved his hands up and down, up and down.

"The giant rock was rolled back. And *an angel* was there. The angel said, 'Jesus is not here. Jesus lives!'"

Then Papa said, "Benjamin, Jesus said that he would be crucified and on the third day he would live again."

Was it true?
Was Jesus alive?

The tall merchant had more to tell. "The women were afraid of the angel and ran away. They ran right into the gardener, but it wasn't the gardener—it was Jesus."

The tall merchant was now laughing. "The women screamed. They shouted for joy. They fell to their knees.

"Do you know what Jesus said?" shouted the tall merchant, jumping up and down. " 'Tell my friends that I am alive,' Jesus said. 'Tell them what you have seen and heard.' "

I too will tell what I have seen and heard.

Days later, Papa and I were walking with the fat merchant on the road to Emmaus. A stranger joined us. Papa told the stranger about Jesus. He told him about the earthquakes, the crucifixion, and the angel.

Then the man placed his hand on my shoulder. He whispered, "Benjamin, I go to my Father in heaven. But I will always be with you." It was Jesus! He really was alive, and he was still my friend.

One day I will be with Jesus in heaven.